French Toast
and
Dutch Chocolate

TRINITY LUTHERAN CHURCH
400 West Blvd. South
Elkhart, IN 46514
(219) 522-1491

Karen O'Connor

Illustrated by Glen Meyers

CPH™
SAINT LOUIS

Junk-Food Finders
Little-Kids' Olympics
French Toast and Dutch Chocolate
Service with a Smile

Copyright © 1994 Concordia Publishing House
3558 S. Jefferson Avenue, St. Louis, MO 63118-3968
Manufactured in the United States of America

1   2   3   4   5   6   7   8   9 10   03 02 01 00 99 98 97 96 95 94

For Noah, Johannah, and Jacob

Contents

1 French Toast and Dutch Chocolate   9

2 *Hola* Means *Hello*   19

3 All-God's-Children Parade   29

4 Swiss Miss   41

5 Canadian Cousins   53

1

French Toast and Dutch Chocolate

Iinternational Food Fair." Luke read the sign over a large table in the center of the mall. Moms and dads and kids and old people crowded around. A lady with gray hair was passing out little books. I bet those are cookbooks, Luke thought.

Then he noticed a tall man in cowboy boots and a Western hat. He was stirring something in a big pot. It smelled like chili. A girl wearing wooden shoes and a blue dress with a white apron passed out chocolates from a pretty box.

The smell of tacos and chocolate, coffee and onions, drifted through the air. Luke felt hungry. He was so hungry he almost forgot about the problem sitting on his mind like a big rock.

He had to think of something to share for the Holidays-around-the-World Festival at school. But all the good ones are gone, he thought. His friend Peter chose Christmas in England. And Mary Ann, the girl who sat behind him, picked Easter in Poland. Those are my two favorite holidays, thought Luke. What's left? Thinking about it only made him feel worse. "I'll think about it later," he told himself. "Right now, I'm hungry."

Luke turned toward the tables. "Dad, look," said Luke, tugging on his father's blue jacket. "A food fair. Can we stop? Maybe the snacks are free." Luke grabbed Dad by the hand. Mother and Laura said they wanted to come too.

"That looks interesting. Smells even better," said Dad. "Let's check it out."

Luke and Laura ran ahead. "What's an international food fair?" asked Laura.

Luke wasn't sure, but he didn't want to admit it. "Well, it's a fair—you know like the Halloween Fair at school, except it's not about Halloween. It's about food." Luke liked the sound of his answer.

Laura stopped to tie her pink and white sneakers. "Maybe they have food from different countries," said Laura. "Isn't that what the word international means?"

Luke let out a long stream of air. Why does she ask me when she already knows the answer, he wondered. "Don't ask me," Luke snapped. "You're the walking dictionary in our family."

Laura stood up. Luke saw her wipe her eyes with her sleeve.

He touched Laura's shoulder and spoke in a softer voice. "I'm sorry," he said, "but sometimes you ask the dumbest questions. Who cares what the word means? Let's eat."

Luke looked down the row of tables. He didn't like chili. But he loved chocolate. He walked toward the girl with the wooden shoes. She was still holding the box of chocolates. Her shoes looked like the ones on the postcard Grandma had sent from Holland.

"Would you like a piece of Dutch chocolate?" the girl asked, smiling.

"Sure, thanks," said Luke, and he popped the sweet candy in his mouth.

"We make this chocolate in Holland," said the girl, "but you don't have to go to Holland to get it. You can buy some right here," she said pointing to the boxes on the table behind her.

"Thanks," said Luke. "I'll tell my mom and dad." He grabbed a piece for Laura and one for his mother and father. Then he walked down the aisle to another table. A man in a white apron stood over a small stove making thin pancakes. Luke read the sign above the stove. "Frenchy's Crepes." He wasn't sure how to say the second word. It must be a French word, thought

Luke, if his name is Frenchy. "Mom will know," he said out loud.

"Mom will know what?" his mother asked as she slipped her arm around Luke's shoulder.

Luke jumped. "Gosh, Mom, I didn't see you coming. What are those little pancakes he's making?"

"They're called crepes" she said. "It's a French word for thin rolled pancakes. I ate my first crepe in France when I was a college student."

"They look kind of flat," said Luke. "I'd still be hungry if I ate those."

Mother laughed. "They're usually served for dessert," she said. "They're often filled with jam and covered with powdered sugar. They're delicious."

"I like French toast better," Luke said. He thought about how his mother cut thick slices of French bread and dipped them in a mixture of egg and milk and cinnamon. Then she fried them quickly till they turned light brown. They tasted yummy with hot maple syrup. Just thinking about French toast made Luke hungry again.

"I don't remember seeing French toast on any menu in France," said Mother. "Maybe it's an American recipe with a French name."

Luke and his mother looked around at all the food stands. "There's something for everyone, isn't there?" asked Mother.

"There sure is," said Luke. He pointed to the signs over each table and read them out loud. "Spaghetti. Chow mein. Irish stew. Dutch chocolate. English pudding." Wow! thought Luke. There sure is a lot to learn about other people and other lands.

That reminded Luke of the Holidays-around-the-World Festival at school. The festival's tomorrow, he thought, and I'm still not sure what I'm going to share. Why did I wait so long?

Laura walked over to Luke. She was munching on a Chinese egg roll. "Luke, look at this. It looks like a tiny sleeping bag. It has chopped vegetables inside." Laura held up the egg roll so Luke could take a bite. "Did you ever make these in your Junior Chef Club?"

"No, we didn't. Now stop asking so many questions," he said in a loud voice.

Laura stomped off. "Luke Taylor," she said over her shoulder, "you're the meanest person in the whole world."

Luke felt as small as an ant. It wasn't Laura's fault that he was in a bad mood. It was his fault. He knew that. He was often mean to Laura. And she was right last night when she'd told him he was a lazybones for not doing his homework on time.

Luke shuffled his feet and stuck his hands in his jacket pocket. He took a breath and blew it out slowly.

That's me, he thought, a lazybones. But I don't like being lazy. I better start praying for some help.

"Hi there, young man." A soft voice broke into his thoughts. "Would you like a copy of our free booklet?"

The lady with grey hair held out a box of small paperback books.

Luke picked up a copy. He hoped it was a cookbook so his mom could learn to make all this good food. He read the title to himself—*Fun and Food around the World.* "Hey, this is neat," Luke exclaimed. "Different foods from different places around the world. Thanks," he said.

"You're welcome," said the woman. "You can learn about the food and customs of different lands," she said. "I hope you'll show it to your friends and your teacher too."

"I will," said Luke, "for sure."

Luke found Mom and Dad and Laura and gave them their chocolate. Then he sat down on a bench while Laura and Mother stood in line for a Mexican taco. Dad stood in another line. He wanted to taste Japanese sushi. But not Luke. Raw fish sounded yucky to him.

Luke flipped though the book. Suddenly he stopped on page 34. There across the top of the page he saw the word *LAZYBONES* in big letters. Hey, that's

what Laura called me. But this says *LAZYBONES DAY.*
I wonder what that means, thought Luke.

A picture showed boys and girls running in the street holding pots and pans above their heads. Some children were banging the pots with a spoon. One was knocking on a door. Everyone was smiling. Luke read the page as fast as he could.

LAZYBONES

Are you a lazybones? If you are, you may have to give your friends candy or cake on Lazybones Day. In Holland this is a special day for eating hot cakes with syrup on top. Dutch people call this treat Lazybones Cake.

Early in the morning on this holiday, boys and girls march through the streets. They make as much noise as possible. They shout. They whistle. They bang on pots and pans and they ring doorbells. When they find a boy or girl still sleeping, they shout, "Lazybones, lazybones, tucked in his bed!" The sleepyhead must pay for being a lazybones by giving the boys and girls candy or cake. When everyone is awake, they all go to the market and eat gingerbread, ice cream, and lazybones cake.

Luke chuckled. Wait till I show this to Laura, he thought. I better watch out or she'll want me to give her cake or candy when she catches me sleeping late or not doing my homework.

But deep inside Luke knew that being lazy was not funny. He had a big project due at school and he hadn't even started it yet.

Luke closed the book and let out a long breath. "I have to think of a holiday from another country," he said. "What should I do?" Then suddenly, an idea flashed across Luke's mind. Hey, wait a minute. Lazybones Day is a holiday. It says so right here in this book. And the lady even told me to share it with my friends and teacher. "All right!" Luke said out loud. "I'll have something to share after all."

He could show the picture of this Dutch holiday and explain how it works. And maybe he could even bring in some hot cakes and syrup to share with the class.

"Since I'm a lazybones," he said, laughing, "I guess I have to pay with candy and cake."

Luke closed the book. He felt much better. Just then Mom and Dad and Laura walked over to him.

"Guess what?" he said. "I've decided what I'm going to share at the festival. Listen to this. A long time ago a watchman named Piet Lak fell asleep while enemies marched into Holland. After that, everyone called

Piet 'Lazy Lak.'" Then Luke told them how Dutch children celebrate Lazybones Day.

"Golly, Luke, how did you learn so much so fast?" Laura's eyes opened wide.

Luke opened the book to page 34 and showed Laura and Mother and Dad the picture.

"I'll bet you did your homework faster than anyone I know, even me," she said.

Luke laughed and whispered a little prayer of thanks. "And, God, help me not be a lazybones anymore," he said.

Show this story to your school teacher, Sunday school teacher, or your family. Then ask them to help you celebrate Lazybones Day as Luke did. Tell your classmates or family what children in Holland do on this holiday. Act out the customs in a skit. Some children can bang pots and pans. Others can be the sleepyheads. Afterwards, serve Lazybones Cake. To make Lazybones Cake, use any recipe for hot cakes, or follow the directions on a box of pancake mix. Serve with ice cream and warm syrup.

2

Hola Means *Hello*

Luke looked out the window of the church bus. Dust swirled across the road as Mr. Rodriguez pulled into the long driveway that led to the orphanage. Luke knew that an orphanage was a home for kids without a mom and dad. He couldn't imagine not living with his mom and dad and sister. He wondered what it would be like to talk and play with these children.

It had been a long ride—over two hours from San Clemente, California, to Rosarito Beach, Mexico. Luke felt hot and sweaty and thirsty.

Brown-faced boys and girls crowded in front of the bus. Mr. Rodriguez leaned on the horn. Some of the children scooted out of the way. Others kept walking toward the bus. They laughed and talked, but Luke couldn't understand what they were saying.

This is terrible, he thought. Our class is going to be here all day and I won't be able to say one word. Miss

19

Hanley had taught the Sunday school class a few Spanish words to get ready for their visit to the orphanage. But now Luke was so nervous he couldn't remember even one.

He tried to say the words on the wooden sign by the gate, but they wouldn't come out. I bet Alberto will know, thought Luke. His grandma was born in Mexico. He and his dad spoke Spanish at home. Luke leaned over to his seat partner. "What does that sign say?"

"Orfanatorio del Norte," said Alberto.

Luke sat up straight and blinked his eyes. "Wow," he said, "you sure speak good Spanish."

Alberto laughed. "It's easy. My father and grandma and grandpa speak it all the time."

Mr. Rodriguez turned from the driver's seat and winked at Luke and his son, Alberto. "Luke, did you know Alberto learned Spanish before he learned English?"

"No, I didn't. That's neat. What do the words mean?" asked Luke.

Alberto smiled proudly. "The North Orphanage," he said. "Dad said there's another one in the south part of town. It's called Orfanatorio del Sur."

Luke admired Alberto. He wished he could speak two languages.

"Do you want me to teach you some Spanish words?" asked Alberto, as Mr. Rodriguez parked the bus.

"That'd be great," said Luke with a sigh. He suddenly felt better. "I was getting real scared," he admitted. "I thought maybe I should stay in the bus all day."

"No way, José," said Alberto, laughing. "Stick with me. I'll help you."

Luke followed his partner to the front of the bus. "Gee thanks," he said. Then Luke and Alberto jumped down the step into the parking lot.

Luke watched Alberto run over to a group of boys playing catch.

"Hola!" he said. "Como se llama? Me llamo Alberto."

All the boys seemed to answer at once. Luke had never heard some of the names before—Carlos, Eduardo, Antonio, Thomas, and Arturo. Carlos and Eduardo sounded a little bit like American names to Luke. I wonder if they mean Carl and Edward. Luke decided to ask Alberto.

Gosh, he thought, I'll never remember all these names. And what can I say to these boys? I don't even know how to ask them to play catch. I wish I'd stayed home.

Then Luke saw Alberto pointing at him. He said something to the boys. They laughed and cheered and bumped each other in the shoulder. "Amigo. Amigo," a tall thin boy said as he walked up to Luke. Next, all the boys crowded around Luke and started talking at once. Luke felt his face turn warm. He remembered that the word *amigo* means friend.

Alberto grabbed Luke by the arm and smiled. "I asked them their names and I told them mine. Then I told them your name is Luke and that we're friends—amigos—in Sunday school."

"Hey, I was right," said Luke proudly. "But why is that boy calling me friend?" asked Luke. "He doesn't even know me."

"You're a new friend," said Alberto. "They all think you're great. I told them you're a junior chef and you play soccer and you won a prize at the Holiday Festival."

Luke gulped hard. "Gosh, Alberto, thanks." Luke didn't know what to do next. The boys stood there, smiling, and tossing a torn baseball to one another. Two younger boys kicked an old can across the driveway.

Then suddenly a little girl ran over to Luke and pulled him by the hand. "Ven a ver mi perro," she called. Luke dragged his feet. He didn't know what she was saying or where she was taking him.

Alberto laughed and pushed Luke from behind. "She wants you to see the new dog," he said. "*Perro* means *dog*."

Luke smiled. "Okay," he said.

The little girl with large brown eyes looked about three years old.

"Como se llama?" Luke squeaked out the words Alberto had taught him.

"Veronica," the girl said softly.

Luke pointed to himself. "Luke," he said. "Me llamo Luke."

Suddenly Luke felt something nipping at his shoe. He looked down at the cutest, fluffiest little puppy he had ever seen. Luke picked up the puppy and stroked its soft fur. The dog licked Luke's hand. Veronica looked up and smiled.

"Eres tu mi amigo Americano?" she asked.

Luke didn't understand all the words she said. But he was pretty sure she wanted to know if he was her friend from America.

"Si, Veronica. I'm your friend. And you're *my* friend too."

Luke put down the wiggling dog and waved to Veronica as she ran after the new pet.

Luke suddenly felt small and humble. "Gosh, Lord," he prayed quietly. "These kids hardly have anything. An old ball that's no good, some dirty cans to kick around. And look at their clothes and shoes. It must be terrible growing up without a mom and dad. I'd never want to live in an orphanage." Luke wiped his nose with his sleeve. Tears came into his eyes as he looked at the play area made of dirt. Even the tree looked small and lonely.

Two women held babies on their laps. An older man carried a big jug of milk up some broken steps. Bees buzzed around a little girl who sat drawing in the dirt with a stick.

Luke thought about his nice bike, his closet full of clothes, his sister Laura, and Mom and Dad. They had a nice house. He had his own room. They were together. And they had everything they needed.

Just then Miss Hanley clapped her hands. She and Mr. Rodriguez told the Sunday school children that it was time to go inside for crafts. The teacher carried a big box with yarn, crayons, colored paper and pencils, scissors, and some storybooks in Spanish.

"I'd like each of you to ask one of the Mexican children to be your partner," said Miss Hanley.

"We're going to show them how to make yarn dolls and finger puppets," said Mr. Rodriguez. "This might be the first toy some of these children ever had."

Luke didn't know what to say or whom to ask to be his partner. He looked around for Alberto. He needed his friend to speak for him. But Luke didn't see him anywhere. He punched his right fist into his left hand and dug his shoe into the dirt. "Great," he said. "Just great. He told me to stick with him and now he's gone when I need him the most."

Just then Luke noticed the thin boy standing alone on the dirt mound. He tossed the torn baseball up in the air and caught it over and over. All the other boys and girls had run off to the playroom. But Eduardo hung back. He kept tossing the ball and catching it.

Luke could feel his heart pounding. He wanted to invite Eduardo to be his partner at crafts. But he didn't know what words to use. He seemed to forget everything Alberto and Miss Hanley had taught him.

I've got to try something, thought Luke. If I don't help Eduardo make a finger puppet, he'll be the only kid without a toy. That would be terrible.

Luke walked over to the dirt mound. His heart pounded so hard he thought it would burst. "Hola, Eduardo." The words came out so easy that Luke surprised himself! Hey that's right, he thought. Hola means hello. We both understand that.

Eduardo smiled. Then he tossed the ball to Luke. Luke caught the ball and tossed it back. Pretty soon they were both laughing and shouting and throwing the ball faster and faster.

Luke could tell that Eduardo liked him. And he hoped Eduardo knew that Luke liked him too. Luke pointed to the playroom. Then he pointed to Eduardo and to himself. He hoped Eduardo would know that he was trying to invite him to be his partner.

Eduardo tucked his T-shirt into his pants. He stamped the dirt from his shoes and ran a hand through his damp hair. He started walking toward the playroom.

He wants to go with me, thought Luke. He knows I want him to be my partner. Luke pulled Eduardo by the sleeve and ran toward the playroom. Eduardo ran alongside him, with the biggest smile Luke had seen all day.

Gee, thanks Lord, Luke prayed, as he climbed the steps of the building. I guess I didn't need Alberto after all. You took care of everything. I don't need to speak Spanish to make a friend. A smile, a hello, and a game of catch are the same in Mexico and America.

MIX AND MATCH

Test your Spanish. Match the words in Column A with the words in Column B. If you don't remember the meaning, look at the story again.

Column A	*Column B*
Eduardo	north
hola	American
amigo	orphanage
Americano	Edward
orfanatorio	hello
norte	friend

3

All-God's-Children Parade

Luke dragged his feet as he walked down the sidewalk to Mom's car in the church parking lot. He wished Laura wasn't so bubbly. He was in a bad mood and it didn't help to see her skipping.

Luke felt angry. Miss Hanley wasn't fair. He had waved his hand high when she asked who wanted to dress like a person from Mexico for the All-God's-Children Parade. But she picked Hector instead. Fine, thought Luke. I'll pretend I'm sick. I'm not going to be in the parade if I can't dress the way I want.

"Mom, guess what?" Laura shouted as she and Luke reached the car. "All the Sunday school classes are having a parade on Saturday. We're celebrating International Day of Prayer."

Laura slid into the front seat. Luke plopped in the back seat. He noticed a puzzled look on his mother's

face. "A parade?" she asked. "It sounds like fun, but what does a parade have to do with praying?"

Laura answered before Luke had a chance to think. "Our teacher said it would be easier for us to pray for people in other countries if we know more about them."

Laura took a deep breath. Then she sipped the apple juice Mother handed her. "We're going to dress up like people from Mexico or Holland or China," said Laura. "Everyone in Sunday school can be in it."

Luke folded his arms across his chest. He shook his head no when Mother handed him a carton of juice.

"What a lovely way to think about it," said Mother, smiling. "Mrs. Schubert comes up with some fine ideas."

Laura twirled a little rubber ball on top of her Bible. "She has a hard time praying for people in other countries because they seem so far away," said Laura. "She thought kids would have a hard time too."

"I think she's right," said Mother. "I just never thought about it before now."

Laura held up a paper that told about the parade. "We can each dress like a person from one of the countries on the list. I want to be a little Dutch girl—like the girl who gave out chocolate at the mall," said Laura.

"We'll march around the playground and around the church parking lot," she said, pointing as they drove away. After the parade we're going to pray for people around the world."

Laura sounded excited. She talked so fast Luke could hardly understand her. "Afterwards some of the kids will share about the country they picked," she said. "There's going to be a microphone on the steps in front of the Sunday school building so everyone can hear."

"Can Daddy and I come?" asked Mother.

"Yes," said Luke in a low voice.

"Well, good, because we wouldn't want to miss it. You can tell Daddy about it when he comes home from church. Right now he's helping count the money from the offering."

Mother glanced over her shoulder, then checked for cars. Luke knew she was looking at him through the little mirror. "What about you, Luke? What country will you represent?"

"I'm not going to be in it," he said. "And it's all Miss Hanley's fault. She plays favorites."

Mother started the car and drove to the exit. "Can you tell me more?" she asked.

Luke felt like crying. But he wanted to tell Mother and Laura how unfair Miss Hanley was. "When she called out Mexico, I raised my hand first," said Luke. "But she let Hector have it instead. He doesn't speak English too well. She said it would be easier for him to dress up like someone from Mexico since he was born there."

Mother stopped at the stoplight and turned to Luke. She reached over the seat and patted his leg.

"I can see you're disappointed," she said. "I know how much you like Mexico, especially after the trip to the orphanage."

Laura popped up from the front seat. "And you could have used Grandpa's big straw hat. It's called a sombrero, remember?"

"I know what a sombrero is, Miss Spanish Dictionary," Luke snapped. "You don't have to tell me again."

Laura sank down in her seat. Mother continued driving. And Luke felt mad. He couldn't help it. It was all Miss Hanley's fault.

"I know you're angry," said Mother as she turned the corner to their street. "But I don't think she meant to hurt your feelings. Hector's a new student. Miss Hanley just wanted to include him."

Laura popped up again. "You could choose another country," she said with a big smile.

"Laura," said Luke in a mean voice. "I know that. Kevin told me the same thing and so did Monica and Matt. But I don't *want* to choose another country. I *want* Mexico. I raised my hand first."

Mother pulled into the driveway and Luke got out of the car slowly. His friend Kevin was waiting by the door. "What are you doing here?" asked Luke with a frown.

"Luke," Mother said with a stern look. "That's not a very friendly greeting. Let's invite Kevin in."

Luke didn't want to be with Kevin or Mom or Laura or anyone. He wanted to be alone.

"Kevin," said Mother. "We're going to have lunch. Would you like to eat with us?"

"Sure, Mrs. Taylor, thanks," said Kevin as he followed Mother and Laura inside.

Luke stood on the front step for a minute longer. Then he walked into the kitchen. He listened as Kevin asked his mom if he could borrow a French hat and a peasant shirt for the parade.

"I'm going to be a French painter," said Kevin. "My grandmother has a paintbrush and a palette I can use." Kevin dabbed the air with his fingers, as if he were painting. Laura and Mother laughed. Luke didn't think it was funny.

Luke noticed Kevin looking right at him. "Do you know what *palette* means?" he asked. But he didn't wait for an answer.

"It's a French word," Kevin said proudly. "A palette is a thin board an artist holds in his hand. He mixes his paints on it. My grandma told me."

Mother pulled a bowl of fruit from the refrigerator and then asked Luke and Laura to set the table. "Have a seat, Kevin," she said. "I used to speak a little French when I was a college student."

She put out a pitcher of juice. "And yes, you can borrow my shirt and hat," she said. "I haven't worn either one of them for years. But Kevin," she asked, "how did you know I had them?"

Kevin sat down at the table. "My mom told me," he said. "You wore the shirt to a costume party once and she remembered it."

"Of course," said Mother laughing. "I forgot all about that. Well, isn't that just like the Lord. He has a place for everything. I often thought of throwing out that old shirt," Mother said, leaning back in her chair. "But I have good memories of wearing it while I lived in France. Now you can use it."

Mother looked at Luke. "Luke, why don't you lead our table prayer." They all folded their hands and said "Amen" after Luke's prayer. Then mother passed a plate of bread and cheese.

Luke watched as Mother put a slice of cheese on the dark bread. Then she spread a bit of mustard on top. Luke could feel his stomach rumble. He was hungry, but he felt too upset to eat. That prayer didn't make me feel better, he thought.

"My shirt and hat are in a big box in the hall closet," Mother said. "We'll take it down as soon as we finish lunch."

Luke felt jealous. Kevin was getting all his mother's attention. I think she likes Kevin better than me, thought Luke. I don't see her helping me with a costume.

Suddenly Luke felt his mother's soft hand on his face. "Mother to Luke, Mother to Luke," she said, smiling. "Is anybody home?"

"Yeah, I'm home," said Luke, slumping down in his seat.

"I need your help," she said. "Let's get that big box down for Kevin. I haven't looked inside it in years. Maybe there are some other interesting things in it."

Laura spun her chair around and hopped off. "Really?" she asked. "What kind of things?"

"Well, I'm not sure," said Mother. She wiped her mouth with a napkin and got up from the table. "Let's find out."

Luke followed Mother and Laura and Kevin to the hall closet. He pulled out the stepstool and climbed up to the top.

"Can you reach it?" asked Mother. "Scoot it out to the edge. Then tip it down and I'll catch it."

Luke moved the box and Mother grabbed it, but the lid slid off. Suddenly the floor was covered with clothes and hats and shoes and some old yellow papers.

Luke noticed that his mother stopped talking as she sorted through the pile of stuff on the floor.

"Look," said Laura. She held up a pair of short leather pants with matching suspenders. "These are neat," she said. "And look at these fancy socks and this little hat. It has a feather." Laura stroked it softly.

Luke wondered where that funny outfit came from, but he didn't want to ask. He was still in a bad mood.

Mother reached for the short pants and suddenly her eyes were wet. Luke thought she was going to cry.

"Oh my," Mother said, and sat back on her heels. "My grandfather's *lederhosen*. And his socks and hat. I haven't looked at these treasures in a very long time."

Luke felt Mother's eyes on him. "Luke, my grandfather was probably about your age when he last wore these. My mother saved them all these years and then passed them on to me. My *grossvater* died when my mother was only 18, so I never knew him."

"What's that funny word you said?" asked Laura.

"*Grossvater*," said Mother. "It means *grandfather* in German."

"I want to try and say it," said Laura. She grabbed the leather pants. "These lederhosen belonged to your grossvater, right?" asked Laura giggling.

"Very good," said Mother. "You get an A+ in German!" she said laughing.

Luke picked up the little green hat and put it on just for fun. It fit! He could hardly believe it. Then he reached for the leather pants and the green and red socks. It was hard to imagine any boy wearing such an outfit. But it did seem special that he had something to remind him of his great-grandfather. He remembered seeing a picture of him as a little boy. Maybe he was wearing those pants in the picture, thought Luke.

Suddenly he got a wonderful idea. He jumped up and grabbed the socks, the pants, the hat, and the suspenders. Then he ran into his room. "I'll be right back," he shouted.

A few minutes later Luke walked into the hall wearing his great-grandfather's clothes. The lederhosen were a bit large, but the hat felt right, and the socks were the right size too. Now all he needed was a shirt and some shoes and he could be in the parade after all. He would be a German boy.

Mother started crying when she saw him. "Oh, Luke, you look wonderful," she said, dabbing her eyes with the corner of her T-shirt. I must take a picture of you to show Grandma. I know she'll cry too."

Luke didn't know what to say. His heart was so full that he felt like crying too. He remembered his mother's words. "The Lord has a place for everything."

Now Luke could see how true that was. God had a place for Hector in the parade. And He has a place for me too, thought Luke. "Thank you, Jesus," he whispered, "for always taking care of me."

Draw a circle around the correct answer. Look back in the story for help.

1. *Lederhosen:*

    big hats

    short leather pants

    long skirts

2. *Sombrero:*

    toy

    a Mexican hat

    shoe

3. *Crepes:*

    French pancakes

    candy

    apples

4. *Grossvater:*

    grandmother

    sister

    grandfather

5. *Palette:*

    paintboard

    food

    game

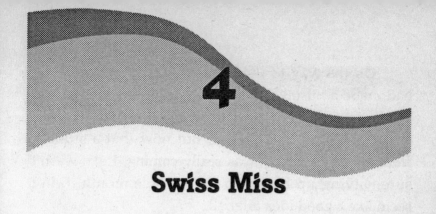

4

Swiss Miss

Luke, Laura." Luke heard his dad call from the family room.

"Hurry! The students from Switzerland will be arriving in an hour. We need to leave for the airport right now."

"Coming," Luke shouted as he grabbed his baseball cap.

"Me too," echoed Laura.

Luke stopped outside his bedroom. He looked at the sign on the door. "Welcome, Susanna!" it said in big letters.

"I'm excited," said Laura. "I hope she's pretty."

"Who cares if she's pretty," said Luke. "I just hope she doesn't mess up my room."

Laura poked Luke in the shoulder. "Gosh, you sure are cranky. Mother said we need to be nice so she'll feel welcome."

On the way to the airport Luke wondered if he had made a mistake. It had been Mother's idea to join the Foreign Student Host Program at church. He and Laura and Dad had agreed. But now that a student from another country was really coming, Luke wasn't sure. Giving up his room for a whole month didn't seem like a good idea after all.

When they arrived at the airport Dad pulled up in front of a sign that said Swiss Air. Then he leaned over the car seat and looked at Luke and Laura. Luke noticed the serious look on his face. "Please be patient and polite," he said. "Susanna will be tired after her long trip from Switzerland. And she may not speak English very well."

Luke's mother opened the car door and got out. "I'll go in and meet her," she said. "The students should be waiting by the information booth."

Luke looked at his watch. Dad turned on the radio. And Laura played with a little doll. A few minutes later Mother walked out the door with a tall girl. Her light brown hair reminded Luke of the color of honey. She wore jeans and a T-shirt, and she carried a backpack.

"Gosh, she seems like a regular girl," said Laura. "She's not wearing one of those costumes like the children in the cuckoo clock."

Luke laughed for the first time that afternoon. "Laura, she wouldn't wear a costume on an airplane.

That would be weird. They only wear them for parades and stuff like that."

"Okay Mr. Know-it-all, Luke Taylor," Laura snapped.

Luke saw his sister's face turn red. Dad frowned at Luke. He was just about to tell Laura he was sorry when Mother opened the car door. Susanna slid in next to Luke and Laura as Mother introduced them.

"What's that pretty box you're holding?" asked Laura.

Susanna smiled. "I have present from my family. You like chocolate?"

She talks kind of funny, thought Luke. Then he remembered that Dad said she was coming to the United States to learn more English.

"I love chocolate," said Laura. "Luke does too." Laura twirled her doll around in her hand. "But we don't eat too much 'cause we're health nuts."

Luke sank down in the seat. He saw Mother cover her mouth with her hand and look over at Dad.

Susanna frowned. "Health nut? I don't understand," she said.

Mother turned to Susanna and spoke slowly. "In America it's a funny name for people who eat natural foods," she said smiling. "Not all Americans eat hamburgers."

Susanna smiled and shook her head. "Ah! A health nut not eat much chocolate, right? Better to eat salad?"

Luke sat up straight and listened. Wow! he thought. She understands English pretty well.

Susanna handed the box to Laura. "Is okay you don't eat. Just look at pictures of my country."

Luke saw that each piece of chocolate was wrapped in a paper with a drawing on it. "It's like a map," said Luke. "All the chocolates together make a big picture of Switzerland. Cool!"

Susanna pointed to one wrapper. "Zurich," she said, "is big city near my village. I live in Baden." Luke listened as Susanna pointed to each piece and said the name of a town in Switzerland.

Dad drove into the driveway just as Susanna pointed to the last picture.

"Luke, will you show Susanna to her room?" asked Dad. "I'll bring her suitcase."

"And Laura," said Mother, "you can show Susanna the bathroom. And maybe she'd like to meet Cocoa."

"Cocoa?" Susanna looked puzzled. "A chocolate drink?" Susanna asked, as she slid out of the car.

Luke covered his mouth. He didn't want to laugh at their new guest.

"Yes," said Mother, "cocoa is a drink. But in our house Cocoa is the name of our pet hamster."

Susanna looked even more puzzled. Luke sighed. Oh boy, he thought. This might be hard. We have to talk real slow. And we have to tell her stuff she doesn't understand. I wish we could just talk like normal people.

Luke held the door for Susanna. Laura led her into the family room. "There's Cocoa," she said, pointing to the cage in the corner.

"Ah!" said Susanna, laughing. "The color is like cocoa."

Laura jumped up and clapped her hands. She turned to Luke. "She understands. This is going to be fun, right Luke?"

Luke wasn't so sure. "Come on, Susanna," he said and led her up the stairs to her room. Laura followed. "This is really my room," he said proudly, as he pushed open the door. "But I said you could stay here and I'll share Laura's room."

"*Danke schön,*" Susanna said. Then she giggled and put her hand over her mouth. "I must speak English, not German. Thank you very much."

"*Danke schön.*" Laura said the same words.

Susanna patted her on the back. "This means *many thanks,*" she said.

Dad walked in with Susanna's suitcase. Mother carried a small box. "Laura and Luke," he said, "did you know that in Switzerland people speak many different languages? Some people speak German, like Susanna. Some speak French. And some speak Italian."

"Why don't they speak Switzerland talk?" asked Laura.

Dad spoke up as he put Susanna's suitcase next to the closet. "Swiss people do have a special language of their own. It's called Swiss German. It sounds a little like German. Most of the families speak it in their homes and villages. But they speak German at work and in school."

Luke wanted to say thank you in German just like Laura. But he was too embarrassed. I'm going to practice first, he told himself. He watched as Mother opened the closet door. She had cleared a space for Susanna's clothes and shoes.

Suddenly Luke frowned. A whole month, he thought. I won't be able to sleep in here for a whole month. What if Susanna breaks something? Or what if she looks in my desk, or takes money out of my piggy bank? The more questions he asked himself, the worse he felt.

Then he remembered something his grandma had taught him about Jesus. "The Lord loves a cheerful giver," she had said. Luke did not feel cheerful about giving his room to this new girl.

"Luke, Laura," Dad said as he walked out of the room with Mother. "Give Susanna some time to put her things away. We'll have lunch in 10 minutes. Wash up, please."

Luke didn't want to wash up. He didn't feel hungry. He wanted to stay near his room and make sure Susanna didn't mess it up. "Luke, I need your help," Mother called.

"Okay," said Luke. He washed his hands and walked downstairs slowly. Mother handed him a basket of warm cornbread. He set it on the table and put out the plates and forks. Everyone sat down. Dad said a prayer. Then Mother passed the rice and black-bean salad.

Susanna sat next to Luke. Oh great, he thought. Is she going to hang around me for a whole month? She sat next to me in the car. She has my room, and now she sits by me at the table.

Luke wished Susanna would go back to Switzerland. Having a student in their house did not feel good. Luke began thinking about his games under the bed. Then he remembered his miniature car collection in the closet. And what about all his books and posters? Would Susanna snoop around his stuff like his cousin Joey did last summer?

Suddenly Luke felt Susanna looking at him. "You want to see?" she asked. "My children." Luke looked at the photographs Susanna held out to him. A group of little boys and girls were painting in a classroom.

Susanna stood in front of the room. She wore a blue and white apron.

Gosh, that's a lot of kids for one lady, thought Luke.

"Where's your husband?" asked Laura.

Susanna laughed softly. Luke sank down in his chair. He was glad Laura asked the question and not him.

"I help the teacher in kindergarten," she said. "No husband. I study to be teacher."

Laura laughed too. "But you said they were your children, so I thought . . . . " Laura's face turned red. She didn't finish her sentence.

Luke sat up and picked at his salad. Boy this is going to be hard, he thought. We're all getting mixed up when we talk.

Luke decided to listen. He didn't want his face to turn red like Laura's. Mother and Dad and Susanna spoke as they ate.

After lunch, Luke pushed his chair away from the table. He looked at Mom and Dad. "I'm going outside, okay?" he asked. He wanted to be with his friends. He wanted to talk with people who could understand him.

Before Mom and Dad could answer, Susanna looked at him again. "Wait, please," she said. "I have present."

Luke felt his heart pound. Gosh, she has a present for me?

Susanna pulled out a small box from her pocket and handed it to Luke.

He tore off the paper and opened the box. A small red pocket knife! "Wow!" Luke didn't know what else to say. He looked at Dad. "My own knife for camping and Scouts," he said. "This is neat."

"It's not just any knife," said Dad. "It's a Swiss Army knife. Look," he said, pointing to the paper that came with the knife. The picture of the knife showed a built-in scissors and a can opener and even a little saw.

Luke could hardly believe it. He had wanted his own knife for a long time. Dad said he might get one for his next birthday. But here it was. Susanna had brought it all the way from Switzerland.

Then she turned to Laura and held out a little bag. Inside was a small doll dressed in a Swiss costume. Luke watched as Laura touched the red skirt and the yellow apron and the white blouse with puffy sleeves. Laura held up the doll for everyone to see. "She's beautiful! I'm going to name her Susanna," said Laura.

Luke suddenly felt ashamed. Gosh, he thought, Susanna sure is a cheerful giver. I didn't want her to use my room. I didn't like talking slow. I didn't want her sitting next to me. But she gave me a present anyway. Luke wished he had a present for her.

Then he remembered what else Grandma had told him. "Jesus is the most cheerful giver of all. He gave His own life to take our sins away."

Luke decided to ask Jesus for help. Jesus, he prayed in his heart, I really need to start over with Susanna. I'm sorry for my mean thoughts. Please take them away and help me. Amen.

Suddenly Luke heard Mother speaking. "These are wonderful presents, Susanna. You know what children like."

Laura jumped up from her seat and gave Susanna a big hug. "Thank you," she said.

Luke felt his heart pounding. He knew that Jesus would help him start over. He tuned to Susanna. "Danke schön," he said softly.

"You welcome," she said, smiling. "Danke schön for present you give me."

Luke wrinkled his nose. What present? he wondered. Maybe Mother had given her a present from the whole family that he didn't know about.

Susanna patted his hand and smiled. "You give me your room. The best present," she said.

Luke let out a deep breath. He knew this was going to be a good month after all.

Share this story with your family and Sunday school teacher. Ask them to find out about foreign students in your town. Maybe your teacher or parents could invite a foreign student to speak to your class or to have dinner at your house. It might also be possible for your family to host a foreign student.

Look in the children's section of your local library for books about people from other lands. Read one and report on it to your family or friends.

5

Canadian Cousins

Luke pulled his green duffel bag out of the closet. Then he piled in his shorts and shirts and tennis shoes. "I'm all set for Vancouver, Canada," he said out loud. "Dad said it's going to be a real adventure."

"Who are you talking to?" Laura asked. She stood in the doorway to Luke's room. She dragged her duffel bag behind her.

"Um, no one," Luke mumbled. He could feel his face get warm. He thought it was weird when he caught Laura talking to herself. Now she caught him. He laughed. Then Laura laughed too. She fell across his bed and propped her chin up with her hands.

"I'm excited, aren't you?" she asked. "This will be our first trip to Canada."

"Yeah, but I'm kind of scared to meet our cousins," said Luke. "What if we don't like them?"

"Maybe they won't like us either," said Laura.

Luke hadn't thought about that. Gosh, that would be terrible. It wasn't fun to play with kids who didn't like you.

Laura rolled over and sat up. She tucked her Minnie Mouse shirt into her blue shorts. "I can't remember our cousins' names," she said.

"Richard, Sharon, and Diane," said Luke.

"Now I remember," said Laura. "And their mom and dad are Aunt Lois and Uncle Paul. Uncle Paul is Daddy's brother, right?"

"Right," said Luke. He stuck one of his baseball caps in the duffel bag. Then he grabbed a sweatshirt and stuffed that in too. It said Vancouver Canucks on the front. Aunt Lois had sent it for his birthday last year. She knew he liked to watch hockey. And the Canucks were one of the most famous hockey teams in the world.

Laura broke into Luke's thoughts. "How come we never saw our cousins before?" asked Laura.

Luke pointed to the world map on the wall over his desk. " 'Cause they lived in England," he said.

"Now I remember," said Laura. "England is all the way across the Atlantic Ocean, right?" She jumped up and ran her finger over the ocean on the map.

"Right," said Luke. "Uncle Paul and Aunt Lois taught school there. All their kids were born in England."

Laura giggled. "Now I remember," she said. "I think they lived in a big city near the Queen."

"London," said Luke. "That's where they lived. The Queen of England lives in London too." Luke noticed an envelope on his desk. It had his name on it. He picked it up just as he heard the phone ring.

"Now I remember," said Laura.

Luke dropped the envelope on his desk. He ran into the hall to answer the phone.

"Hello. Taylor house. Oh hi, Kevin," he said. He listened as his friend told him about a Sunday school volleyball game at the church playground. The girls and the men teachers would play against the boys and the women teachers. Afterwards they would have a barbecue supper at the beach.

"Hey, that'll be a blast," said Luke. "Miss Hanley will be on our team. All right!" Luke made a high five sign, even though Kevin couldn't see him. Luke said good-bye and hung up the phone. Then he grabbed a pencil and wrote a note on the chalkboard on the wall. "Volleyball game at church. Sunday, July 17."

We'll be home from Canada just in time, thought Luke. Dad said we're coming back on July 16. I wonder if I can practice volleyball in Canada.

"Mom, Dad, guess what?" Luke bounded down the stairs as fast as he could.

Mom turned from the desk in the family room. "I give up," she said. "And Dad's not here. He's at the gas station." She took off her glasses and smiled at Luke. "Tell me—quick," she said. "It sounds exciting."

Luke hopped from one foot to another and talked as fast as he could. He wanted his mother to be excited about the game. But she looked worried instead.

"What's wrong, Mom? Can't I be in the game? I have to. It'll be so much fun. Miss Hanley will be on the same team as Kevin and me."

Mother looked at the calendar on the desk. She moved her pencil along the page. Suddenly she stopped. "Oh dear," she said. "Look here. We'll still be in Canada that day." She turned and faced Luke. "We don't come home until the 19th. That's on Monday—the day after the game."

Luke felt a big pain in the middle of his stomach. "But Mom, Dad said we'd be back on Saturday. Remember? Then he could rest on Sunday before going to work."

"I know, dear," she said. "But all the airplanes were filled on Saturday and Sunday. The weekends are the busiest times. We'll be flying home on Monday now."

Luke plopped down on the sofa next to Cocoa's cage. The hamster made little noises. He stuck his nose through a hole in the cage. Maybe he feels sad for me, thought Luke.

"Mom, I have an idea. Could I stay home with Kevin's family while you and Dad and Laura go to Canada? It's only for two weeks."

Mother walked over and sat down beside him. "Luke Taylor," she said in her serious voice, "absolutely not. We wouldn't think of going without you. We're a family and this is a family vacation."

"But Mom . . ."

"Luke, the answer is no," she said. Then Mother reached out and patted his head. "I know you're disappointed," she said in a soft voice. "But we would miss you, and you would miss a lot of fun. You can play volleyball anytime. This is a special trip—our first visit to Canada and your first time to meet your cousins. We're going to learn so many wonderful new things." She got up from the desk and walked over to the window by the garden.

"Let's put this in the Lord's hands," she said. "He always works everything out for the best." She pointed to the little pine tree near the fence. "Look what He did for that tree. It was such a skinny little thing and now it's growing just fine."

Luke slumped down in his seat. Canada didn't seem exciting anymore. There was nothing more to say. And what if Laura was right? What if Richard and

Sharon and Diane didn't like him? He'd have to miss a great game to play with cousins who didn't even like him.

Luke walked upstairs dragging his feet. He plopped down on his bed. He looked at his duffel bag. Then he saw the book about Canada that Mother had brought home from the library. He kicked it off the bed and pounded his pillow. "It's not fair," he said.

"What's not fair?" asked Laura standing in the doorway. "I heard funny noises in here. What's wrong?"

Luke told her about the game and what Mother said.

"Gosh, Luke. Would you really want to stay home? I'd miss you. I don't want to play with our cousins by myself."

Luke sighed, "Don't worry. I'm coming. I *have* to come."

Laura walked over to Luke's desk. She picked up the envelope with his name on it. "You forgot to open your letter," she said."

Luke reached for the letter and ripped it open. "I wonder who it's from. I don't have a pen-pal." Luke pulled out a letter and a colorful brochure. Something else fell to the floor. Luke bent down and scooped it up. It was a picture of Richard, Sharon, and Diane. On the back it said, "Hi to Luke and Laura from your Canadian cousins."

The brochure said *Come to Vancouver.* Luke turned over the letter. "It's from Richard," he said.

Laura tugged on the letter. "Let me see," she said.

Luke handed her the brochure and the picture. He read the letter to himself. Richard sounded nice. His letter was friendly. Luke turned to Laura. "Richard is excited that we're coming to Vancouver. He and Sharon and Diane have a list of fun things to do. The brochure has pictures of the best places to visit."

Laura stared at the picture of their cousins. "Diane is wearing a Beauty and the Beast shirt like mine," said Laura. "And look at Sharon's hair. It's so long."

Luke looked at Richard. He was smiling too. And behind him on the wall was a poster. It said, *Go! Vancouver Canucks.*

Laura opened the brochure. Luke looked at it with her. He read the words under each picture. "Queen Elizabeth Park. Look, Laura, it has a sunken garden. I hope we go there. And look at this," he said pointing to the picture of Stanley Park. "Maybe we can have a picnic here. It has a beach too."

Laura pointed to another picture. "What's this?" she asked.

"It's a museum for stuff about the sea," said Luke. "Look at this ship. It's called St. Roch."

"I bet it's famous," said Laura.

"I want to go here," said Luke, pointing to a picture of the planetarium. "We can see films about the universe and the stars and planets," he said. "Laura, this is so cool. Richard and Sharon and Diane are lucky to live in Canada. I can't wait to go."

"Really?" Laura blinked her eyes. "But what about the volleyball game?"

Luke stopped for a minute. The game. Hey, that's right. I forgot all about the game. Suddenly a volleyball game with friends didn't seem nearly as important as a vacation with his family. Luke smiled. God sure does make everything work together for good, just like Mom said. "Thank you, Lord," he whispered.

Then Luke reached over and playfully punched Laura's shoulder. "I can play volleyball anytime," he said. "Besides, if I didn't go to Canada, Laura, I'd really miss you."

Ask for information about another country from a travel agent or from the library. Read a book on that country. Learn at least three things about that city or country:

1. What language do the people speak?

2. What kind of sports and games do the children play?

3. What are two places of interest to visit?

Do a report on something you like about that country. Perhaps one day you will be able to visit there.